THE EYES IN THE DARK

MUHAMMAD OMAR QURESHI

Contents

I

The Whispered Legends

As the moon hung low in the sky, casting eerie shadows across the sleepy town of Crestwood, Maine, the group of teenagers made their way through the dimly-lit streets, each step accompanied by a sense of unease. Among them were Emma, a spirited 14-year-old with an insatiable thirst for adventure; Eli, a tall and inquisitive boy of the same age, drawn to the mysteries of crime scenes and investigations; Amelia, a 13-year-old with a keen eye for photography; and Josh, the confident and courageous 15-year-old who led the group with unwavering determination.

Their journey through the quiet streets came to an abrupt halt as they rounded a corner, confronted by a scene straight out of a nightmare. Police tape cordoned off the area, and a cluster of officers moved about, their solemn expressions betraying the gravity of the situation. The group's curiosity piqued, they lingered on the outskirts of the scene, exchanging whispered speculations about the nature of the tragedy that had unfolded before them.

"What do you think happened here?" Josh queried, turning to Eli for insight. Eli's gaze swept over the bloodstained pavement and the telltale signs of struggle evident in the surrounding area. "It's hard to say," he replied solemnly, his analytical mind already piecing together the grim details of the crime. "But whatever transpired, it was certainly not a scene for the faint of heart."

Their clandestine observation was abruptly interrupted by the stern voice of an approaching officer, his flashlight casting harsh beams of light upon their startled faces. With a collective gasp, the group scattered, fleeing in different directions, their hearts pounding with adrenaline-fueled panic.

Amelia hurried home, her footsteps muffled by the stillness of the night as she slipped through the door, hoping to evade her mother's notice. Yet, her efforts were in vain as her mother's stern voice echoed through the hallway, her worry evident in every word.

After a brief but tense exchange, Amelia found herself tasked with assisting her Meemaw in clearing out the cluttered attic—a daunting prospect for any teenager. As they sifted through the forgotten relics of the past, a worn and weathered book caught Amelia's eye, its pages yellowed with age and its cover adorned with cryptic symbols.

Unable to resist the allure of the mysterious tome, Amelia surreptitiously tucked it away in her bag, eager to explore its secrets in the safety of her own room. Later that night, bathed in the soft glow of her bedside lamp, she delved into its pages, her curiosity ignited by the tantalizing promise of forbidden knowledge.

As she read, the hairs on the back of her neck stood on end, each word painting a vivid picture of a malevolent entity known as the Nightstalker—a creature of darkness and shadow, lurking in the depths of the night, its insatiable hunger for blood and violence a chilling reminder of the horrors that lurked beyond the safety of daylight.

Before she could delve any further into the sinister lore of the Nightstalker, she was interrupted by the sound of her mother's approaching footsteps. Hastily concealing the book beneath her pillow, she feigned sleep, her mind racing with thoughts of the terrifying creature that now haunted her dreams.

The following day at school, the group gathered to discuss their latest discovery, the ominous book serving as a grim reminder of the dangers that lurked within the shadows. Yet, their conversation was cut short by the somber announcement of a classmate's untimely demise—a stark reminder of the fragility of life and the ever-present specter of death that loomed over their small town.

Undeterred by the tragedy that had befallen their classmate, the group resolved to uncover the truth behind the mysterious murder that had shaken their community. Armed with determination and a sense of purpose, they prepared to embark on a perilous journey into the heart of darkness, where the secrets of the Nightstalker awaited them.

As night descended upon the town once more, the group gathered outside the abandoned house where the murder had taken place, their nerves steeling themselves for the unknown horrors that awaited them within. With a silent nod of understanding, they set their plan into motion, lowering Josh into the darkness below with a makeshift rope and a series of signals to guide their communication.

Yet, as Josh descended into the depths of the decrepit house, what he encountered within would haunt him for the rest of his days. The sight of a brutally mutilated body, its twisted form a testament to the savage brutality of the Nightstalker, sent waves of nausea coursing through his veins, threatening to overwhelm him with a primal sense of fear and revulsion.

With a series of frantic tugs on the rope, Josh signaled for his friends to pull him to safety, his voice trembling as he recounted the horrors he had witnessed within. As they hastily retreated from the scene, their minds reeling with shock and disbelief, one thing became abundantly clear: the legend of the Nightstalker was no mere myth, but a terrifying reality that threatened to consume them all.

II

The Eyes in the dark

Descending from the house, an officer spotted them, commanding their compliance behind the yellow tape and interrogating them regarding their presence. "Uh...we were merely passing by, and we noticed the police cars...and such, so naturally, we became curious," Emma stuttered nervously, her voice trembling and beads of sweat forming on her brow.

The officer cast a skeptical glance at them and remarked wryly, "Well, curiosity killed the cat, as they say. However, I advise you youngsters to steer clear of places like this in the future. It's not safe."

As they walked away, Eli remarked, "We must uncover more about this Darkstalker guy." "It's the NIGHTSTALKER, not the DARKSTALKER GUY!" corrected Amelia, her tone tinged with mockery directed at Eli.

Resuming from where they had left off, they huddled together, scanning through the pages in search of clues. They stumbled upon a chapter titled "Containment," which immediately captured their attention. It detailed an idol hidden within the expansive forest surrounding the town. Upon this idol lay a spell that needed recitation within the temple of shadows.

Once the incantation was completed, all Nightstalkers would be irresistibly drawn to the idol with an indescribable force, ensnaring them within and bringing an end to the bloodshed.

As night had fallen, the group dispersed, each heading towards their respective homes. While traversing the dimly lit streets, Josh, humming a tune, caught sight of a figure ahead, its silhouette barely discernible in the darkness.

Approaching cautiously, Josh, wary of potential danger, observed the figure, gradually recognizing it as Levi, his younger brother, gazing intently at something in the distance.

"Hey, Levi!" Josh called out, receiving no response as Levi remained fixated on whatever had captured his attention. "What are you doing out here at this hour, Levi?" Josh inquired once more, met with silence. Attempting to draw nearer, Levi turned around, revealing his face to Josh, who was overcome with terror at the sight of Levi's eyes glinting in the night, and a smile so wide which was humanly impossible.

Without hesitation, Josh fled, his heart racing as though it might burst from his chest, his "brother" now pursuing him with unnerving speed, releasing bloodcurdling screams and growling. Racing onward, Josh spotted a nearby gas station still open, darting inside to safety within its bright confines.

As the perplexed cashier questioned Josh about the commotion, Josh pointed frantically to Levi, who stood outside, his eyes still gleaming. However, the cashier dismissed Josh's claims, stating, "Kid, I don't have time for games. There's nothing out there."

III
Shapeshifter?

After the tumultuous events of the previous night, Josh found himself grappling with a whirlwind of emotions as he burst into Levi's room, intent on confronting him about the eerie encounter. However, his resolve crumbled upon finding Levi peacefully asleep, oblivious to the chaos that had unfolded.

Haunted by lingering doubts and fears, Josh tossed and turned in bed, his mind racing with unanswered questions. The morning brought little solace as he awoke to a world still shrouded in uncertainty. Determined to seek answers, he reached out to Eli, whose call for a meeting at the local park after school provided a glimmer of hope amidst the chaos.

As the group gathered at the park, tension hung heavy in the air, each member wrestling with their own apprehensions. Eli wasted no time in delving into the mysterious book, uncovering another chilling detail about the Nightstalker's ability to shapeshift into the likeness of loved ones—a revelation that sent shivers down everyone's spines.

The realization that their own family and friends could potentially be used as pawns by the Nightstalker added a new layer of dread to their already perilous situation. Yet, amidst the fear, a newfound determination emerged as they resolved to put an end to the terror once and for all.

With trembling hands, Josh turned another page of the book, revealing a weathered map hidden within its pages. Its antiquated appearance and the faint scent of aged paper lent an air of mystery to the discovery, capturing their attention in an instant.

Amelia, ever the voice of reason and determination, seized upon the opportunity presented by the map, tracing the pathway to the Shadow Temple hidden deep within the forest. Her proclamation ignited a spark of hope within the group, as they dared to believe that they might finally have a chance to vanquish the Nightstalker and bring peace to their town.

However, the gravity of their decision weighed heavily upon them, as they grappled with the daunting prospect of venturing into the treacherous depths of the forest, where the Nightstalkers roamed freely under the cover of darkness.

Amelia's frustration bubbled to the surface as she confronted the hesitant silence that greeted her rallying cry. With determination blazing in her eyes, she declared her intention to embark on the perilous journey alone, a fierce resolve driving her forward.

Yet, in a moment of solidarity, Eli stepped forward, offering his unwavering support. His gesture sparked a chain reaction, as Josh and Emma, overcome by a shared sense of duty and camaraderie, pledged their allegiance to the cause.

Amidst the group's fervent discussion, the tranquility of the park was shattered by the piercing wails of ambulance and police car sirens slicing through the air. Instantly, their attention was captivated by the urgent cacophony, prompting them to abandon their conversation and follow the convoy of vehicles hurtling towards an undisclosed destination.

With a sense of foreboding hanging heavy in the air, the group trailed behind the speeding cars, their hearts pounding with anticipation and dread. Their journey culminated at the doorstep of Mr. and Mrs. Benson's house, where a grim scene awaited them.

Upon arrival, they were met with the sight of police officers and EMTs swarming the property, their faces etched with grim determination as they prepared to breach the residence. The neighbor's frantic call had alerted authorities to the grisly discovery of blood splattered across the windows, signaling yet another senseless tragedy.

As the officers forced their way into the house, the group watched with a mixture of horror and disbelief as the grim reality of the situation unfolded before their eyes. Mr. and Mrs. Benson, beloved members of the community, had fallen victim to the same gruesome fate that had befallen others in the town—a stark reminder of the merciless reign of terror gripping their once peaceful community.

With each new murder, the spotlight on their small town grew ever brighter, drawing the attention of the media and thrusting their quiet community into the harsh glare of international scrutiny. Yet, amidst the chaos and despair, a steely resolve began to take root within the group.

Realizing that they could no longer afford to remain idle while the Nightstalkers continued their relentless onslaught, they resolved to take action. With determination burning in their hearts, they set about crafting a plan to confront the darkness head-on and put an end to the senseless bloodshed once and for all.

As the first light of dawn cast a faint glow across the horizon, the group stirred from their slumber, each member fueled by a sense of determination and purpose. With quiet resolve, they gathered their supplies, ensuring that they were equipped for the arduous journey that lay ahead.

With backpacks laden with canned food, water bottles, spare clothes, and essential survival gear, the group assembled behind the city's swimming pool, a makeshift rendezvous point chosen for its discreet location and proximity to the forest's edge. Flashlights, compasses, and flares were distributed among them, their presence serving as a beacon of hope amidst the encroaching darkness.

Eli, resolute in his determination to protect his friends, had secured his father's rifle, a symbol of both strength and necessity in the face of imminent danger. With each member accounted for and all preparations in place, the group set forth on their journey into the unknown, their footsteps guided by a shared sense of purpose and camaraderie.

IV
Adventure begins

As the group ventured deeper into the jungle, the dense canopy overhead cast the forest floor into shadow, shrouding their surroundings in an eerie gloom. The rhythmic chirping of unseen insects provided a haunting soundtrack to their journey, punctuated only by the occasional rustle of leaves and the distant calls of wildlife.

Navigating through the labyrinth of tangled foliage proved to be no small feat, as they pushed aside thick vines and skirted around gnarled roots that threatened to trip them at every turn. The air hung heavy with humidity, causing beads of sweat to form on their brows and dampen their clothes despite the early hour.

With Eli leading the way, his father's rifle slung over his shoulder as a silent reminder of the dangers that lurked in the shadows, the group pressed on, their determination unwavering in the face of the unknown. Each step brought them deeper into the heart of the jungle, where the air seemed to grow thicker with each passing moment, as if weighted down by the secrets that lay hidden within its depths.

As the day wore on, fatigue began to set in, the relentless heat sapping their energy and leaving them feeling drained and weary. Yet, they pushed forward, driven by the knowledge that their journey was far from over and that every step brought them closer to their goal.

By midday, the group decided to take a brief respite, pausing to rest and replenish their energy supplies. They found a small clearing amidst the dense foliage, where they could take shelter from the oppressive heat and refuel with water and canned food from their packs.

As they sat in the shade of towering trees, their senses on high alert for any signs of danger, they couldn't help but marvel at the beauty of their surroundings. Sunlight filtered through the dense canopy above, casting dappled patterns of light and shadow on the forest floor below, while the sounds of wildlife echoed in the distance, a testament to the thriving ecosystem that called this place home.

Despite the tranquility of their surroundings, however, a sense of unease lingered in the air, a constant reminder of the dangers that lurked just beyond the edge of their perception. With the sun sinking lower on the horizon, casting long shadows that stretched across the forest floor, the group knew that they could not afford to linger for long.

And so, with renewed determination, they rose to their feet and continued on their journey, their resolve unshaken by the challenges that lay ahead. For as daunting as the path before them may be, they knew that they could not turn back now—not when the fate of their town hung in the balance, and the shadows of the jungle beckoned them ever onward.

As the golden hues of the setting sun painted the sky in vibrant shades of orange and pink, casting long shadows across the jungle floor, the group hurriedly set up their tents, seeking shelter from the encroaching darkness. With the sounds of nocturnal creatures beginning to stir in the underbrush, a palpable sense of unease settled over the camp, prompting them to assign a rotating watch to stand guard throughout the night.

As Emma's turn to keep watch arrived, she reluctantly emerged from the safety of the tent, her fingers trembling as they gripped the cold metal of the rifle. The dense canopy above seemed to swallow the last remnants of daylight, plunging the jungle into an eerie twilight that sent shivers down Emma's spine.

With every rustle of leaves and snap of twigs, her heart raced with anticipation, her senses heightened by the oppressive silence that enveloped the jungle. As she leaned against a tree, exhaustion weighing heavily upon her, her eyelids drooped, and she fought to stay awake, the rhythmic chirping of crickets lulling her into a drowsy haze.

Suddenly, a movement caught her off guard, jolting her awake with a start. In a panic, she raised the rifle and fired blindly into the air, the deafening shots echoing through the stillness of the night. As the echoes faded, Emma's pulse pounded in her ears, her breath coming in ragged gasps as she scanned the darkness for any sign of danger.

But as her eyes adjusted to the dim light, she realized with a wave of relief that the source of the movement was none other than Eli, returning from a brief trip to relieve himself. With an abnormal and uncanny smile, he stood there completely still, staring into nowhere.

As Emma's watch came to an end, she retreated into the tent, eager to seek solace in the company of her friends. But as she called out to the next person to take over guard duty, her voice caught in her throat as she realized that Eli was already nestled snugly among the others, fast asleep.

A chill ran down Emma's spine as she turned her gaze back to the figure standing just beyond the tent, its eyes gleaming in the darkness with an unsettling intensity. Without hesitation, she raised the rifle once more, her hands steady despite the fear coursing through her veins.

But as she took aim and fired, the bullets passed straight through the figure, revealing its true form as a monstrous entity, towering over her with jagged claws and a gaping maw dripping with blood. With a surge of adrenaline, Emma braced herself for the impending attack, her eyes squeezed shut in anticipation of the inevitable.

Yet, as she dared to peek through her lashes, she found the creature looming ominously in the distance, its gaze fixed upon the cross pendant hanging from her neck. With a sense of grim determination, Emma clutched the symbol tightly, knowing that it was her only hope of warding off the darkness that threatened to consume her.

As the first rays of dawn filtered through the dense canopy of the jungle, the intrepid group pressed on with their expedition. With a swift glance at the weathered map and a decisive check of the compass, Emma pointed towards the looming peaks to the east. "There," she declared, her voice steady with determination, "our next trial awaits us beyond those formidable mountains."

As the weary members of the group turned their tired gazes towards Emma, their grumbles and complaints mingled with the rustle of leaves underfoot. Yet, their reverie was abruptly shattered by the distant, rhythmic thrum of helicopter rotors slicing through the humid air. With a sense of urgency, Josh scrambled up a nearby tree, his keen eyes scanning the horizon until he pinpointed the source: a convoy of search and rescue helicopters steadily approaching their location.

Initially puzzled by the unexpected arrival, the realization dawned upon the group like a sudden flash of lightning in the dim forest. They had vanished without a trace, and now the long arm of law enforcement was reaching out to find them. In the midst of the ensuing chaos, Amelia's voice cut through the air like a sharp blade. "We must conceal ourselves from those helicopters at all costs!"

V

Frosty peaks of the East

The group scrambled with urgency, melding seamlessly into the dense foliage of the forest floor, each member moving with the stealth of seasoned hunters. Not a single breath escaped their lips as they nestled themselves under the protective canopy, concealed from prying eyes. They remained frozen in their hiding places, hearts pounding in sync with the rhythmic thud of the helicopter rotors as they passed overhead, the sound gradually fading into the distance as the search continued its northward trajectory.

With the immediate threat of discovery abated, the group resumed their journey through the dwindling forest, the verdant canopy giving way to jagged peaks looming ominously on the horizon, promising a harsh and unforgiving terrain ahead. As the sun dipped low on the horizon, casting a fiery glow over the rugged landscape, the group heeded its silent command to make camp for the night.

Amelia, entrusted with the solemn duty of guarding the tent, accepted the cross pendant from Emma, a talisman against the encroaching darkness that whispered of unseen terrors lurking in the shadows. As night descended like a shroud over the rugged landscape, Josh took up his post, his senses attuned to the myriad sounds of the wilderness.

Suddenly, amidst the symphony of nocturnal noises, a piercing scream shattered the stillness, cutting through the night like a blade. Without hesitation, Josh seized the rifle, his muscles coiled with tension as he raced towards the source of the distress, his breath hanging like mist in the cool night air.

But as he reached the clearing, a chilling realization gripped him like icy tendrils: he had unwittingly stumbled into the clutches of the nightstalkers' trap. A legion of gleaming white eyes surrounded him, closing in with predatory intent, their presence suffusing the darkness with an aura of malevolence.

Frantically searching for the cross pendant, Josh's fingers closed around empty air, his heart sinking as he realized his grave error. Before he could react, a deafening screech rent the air, hurling him backwards with brutal force, his body colliding with the unforgiving bark of a nearby tree.

Struggling to regain his footing, Josh found himself ensnared in the merciless grip of the nightstalkers, their forms closing in with ravenous hunger. Yet, just as all hope seemed lost, a brilliant light pierced the darkness from above, accompanied by the familiar thud of helicopter rotors.

As the celestial glow bathed the clearing in its radiant embrace, the nightstalkers recoiled in terror, vanishing into the shadows from whence they came. With a surge of relief, Josh scrambled back towards the safety of the camp, igniting a blazing campfire to ward off any lingering remnants of the nocturnal horrors that had threatened to consume them.

With the nightstalkers driven back into the depths of the forest, the group gathered their belongings and steeled themselves for the next leg of their perilous journey: the ascent into the unforgiving embrace of the mountains. As dawn painted the sky with hues of pink and gold, they set out with determination etched upon their faces, their footsteps echoing against the rugged terrain.

The once verdant landscape of the forest gave way to rocky slopes and towering peaks, their jagged silhouettes cutting a stark contrast against the azure sky. Every step forward was a test of endurance, the thin mountain air biting at their lungs and the treacherous terrain threatening to betray their footing at any moment.

Yet, amidst the harsh beauty of the mountains, there was a sense of awe and wonder that enveloped the group. They marveled at the sheer majesty of their surroundings, each peak a silent sentinel bearing witness to the passage of time.

As they climbed higher, the temperature dropped, and the air grew thinner still, a reminder of the harsh realities of the mountain wilderness. Yet, with each passing obstacle overcome, their bonds grew stronger, forged in the crucible of adversity.

day turned into night as they pressed ever onward, their determination unyielding in the face of the mountain's relentless assault. They navigated treacherous ridges and icy precipices, their resolve unwavering as they drew closer to their elusive goal.

With a heavy heart and a sense of urgency, Eli ventured forth into the wilderness, his eyes scanning the rugged landscape for any sign of shelter. Every step was fraught with tension, his senses heightened to the threat of the lurking nightstalkers, ready to pounce upon unsuspecting prey.

Suddenly, a piercing scream shattered the stillness of the mountain air, jolting Eli into a state of high alert. Gripping the rifle tightly in trembling hands, he called out nervously, his voice laced with a mixture of fear and determination, demanding the source of the sound to reveal themselves.

As a figure emerged from the snowy depths of a nearby cave, Eli's heart raced with adrenaline-fueled apprehension. The man, clad in a weather-beaten airforce uniform and raising his hands in a gesture of surrender, begged for mercy, his words choked with desperation.

"Who are you?" Eli demanded, his voice echoing against the cavern walls, his gaze unwavering as he sought answers from the stranger before him. Yet, the man remained silent, his expression fraught with an unspoken plea for understanding.

Attempting to calm the tense situation, the man gestured for Eli to lower the rifle, his movements cautious yet deliberate. With a wary eye, Eli approached the stranger, each step measured and deliberate, his senses on high alert for any sign of danger.

"I...uh no speak English," the man muttered, his voice trembling with the chill of the mountain air, his eyes betraying a hint of fear. "I fly...crash...boom...this place."

As Eli's gaze fell upon the red star emblazoned upon the man's uniform, realization dawned upon him. "Soviet?" he questioned, seeking confirmation of the man's origins.

The man nodded solemnly, his features drawn with a mixture of resignation and uncertainty. "Da, ya Kirill," he replied, his voice barely above a whisper, bracing himself for what he believed to be an inevitable confrontation.

However, instead of succumbing to fear and suspicion, Eli extended an unexpected gesture of compassion, inviting Kirill to accompany them to their tent, a beacon of warmth and safety amidst the harsh wilderness.

As they made their way back to the sanctuary of the tent, a cacophony of unearthly screeches shattered the tranquility of the mountain night, heralding the arrival of the dreaded nightstalkers. With a steely resolve, Kirill ordered Eli to flee, his voice ringing with urgency as he prepared to face the oncoming horde alone.

With a heavy heart and tear-filled eyes, Eli obeyed, his footsteps echoing against the rocky terrain as he raced towards safety. Yet, even as he sought refuge within the confines of the tent, the haunting memory of Kirill's sacrifice lingered like a shadow upon his soul, a poignant reminder of the cruel realities of the mountain wilderness.

VI

The Perilous Journey through the mountains

As the sun rose, its golden rays struggled to penetrate the thick, brooding clouds that hung low in the sky like a heavy shroud, casting the landscape into a dim, ominous gloom. The promise of rain loomed large, whispered by the rustle of leaves and the distant rumble of thunder, painting the mountain vista with an air of foreboding.

Undeterred by the bleakness of their surroundings, the group pressed onward through the rugged terrain of the mountains, their resolve unyielding in the face of the lurking dangers that awaited them. No longer confined to the cloak of darkness, the Eyes in the Dark now prowled the mountainside even in the harsh light of day, their malevolent presence palpable in every shadow.

As they drew nearer to the summit, a solitary figure emerged from the haze, a commanding presence clad in the uniform of the United States Air Force, the distinct red star emblazoned upon his helmet a beacon of authority. His voice carried on the wind, booming with an air of enforcement as he called out to the group, urging them to abandon their quest and return home.

Amelia's voice rang out, sharp with suspicion, demanding answers from the enigmatic figure. Yet, as he claimed to be part of the USAF and gestured towards a group of similarly attired individuals, doubt gnawed at the edges of their minds. Could this be a ruse perpetrated by the cunning nightstalkers?

Josh's inquiry sparked a heated debate among the group, their voices rising in discord as they grappled with the possibility of betrayal. But it was Emma's chilling revelation that sent shivers down their spines, her words a damning indictment of the deception before them.

"The USAF doesn't have red stars on their helmets," she declared, her voice laced with a chilling certainty that silenced the group in an instant. In that moment of realization, the facade crumbled, revealing the true nature of their would-be rescuers.

The "USAF" individuals' eyes flickered with an otherworldly glow, their smiles twisted into grotesque caricatures of malice as they closed in on the group, their intentions unmistakably sinister. With a collective gasp, the quartet turned on their heels, their flight spurred by a primal instinct for survival as they fled from the encroaching darkness.

Yet, as they glanced back over their shoulders, the figures were gone, swallowed by the shifting shadows of the mountainside, leaving behind only a lingering sense of dread in their wake. With hearts pounding and adrenaline coursing through their veins, the group pressed on, their journey fraught with peril and uncertainty as they sought to escape the clutches of the insidious nightstalkers.

With each frantic step, the quartet plunged deeper into the heart of the mountains, their breaths ragged and hearts racing in sync with the rhythm of their desperate flight. The oppressive weight of the looming darkness seemed to press down upon them, urging them onward with a sense of urgency born of primal fear.

Eli, his senses heightened by the adrenaline coursing through his veins, cast anxious glances over his shoulder, half-expecting to see the malevolent figures of the nightstalkers looming just behind them. Yet, the mountainside remained eerily silent, save for the distant echo of their own hurried footfalls.

As they traversed treacherous slopes and winding trails, the terrain grew increasingly rugged, each jagged rock and gnarled root a potential obstacle in their path. Yet, fueled by sheer determination and the desperate need to escape their pursuers, they pressed onward, their resolve unyielding despite the daunting challenges that lay ahead.

Amidst the chaos of their flight, a sense of unity emerged within the group, binding them together in a shared struggle against the encroaching darkness. Each member drew strength from the presence of the others, their solidarity a beacon of hope amidst the encroaching gloom.

Yet, as the hours stretched on and exhaustion threatened to overwhelm them, doubts began to creep into their minds. Would they ever find refuge from the relentless pursuit of the nightstalkers? Or were they doomed to wander these unforgiving mountains until their strength failed them?

But even in the face of uncertainty, the quartet refused to succumb to despair, drawing upon reserves of courage and determination they never knew they possessed. With every step forward, they pushed back against the encroaching darkness, their spirits unbroken despite the trials that lay ahead.

As the weary travelers reached the summit, a breathtaking spectacle unfolded before their eyes. The thick, oppressive clouds that had shrouded the sky dispersed like tendrils of mist, yielding to the radiant brilliance of the setting sun. Golden rays cascaded over the rugged peaks, casting a warm, ethereal glow upon the landscape below.

In the fading light of day, the verdant expanse of the jungle stretched out before them like an emerald tapestry, its lush foliage bathed in the soft hues of twilight. Yet, amidst the tranquil beauty of their surroundings, an aura of ancient mystery lingered in the air, whispering of secrets long forgotten and untold dangers lurking in the shadows.

With renewed determination, the group pressed onward, their hearts filled with anticipation as they embarked upon the final leg of their journey. Through dense undergrowth and winding pathways, they forged ahead, each step bringing them closer to their elusive destination: the fabled Shadow Temple.

VII
The Battle of Coyotes

As the group pressed onward through the dense forest, this leg of their journey proved markedly distinct from their previous trials amidst the rugged mountains. Here, amidst the verdant foliage, danger lay concealed within the very shadows they traversed. As they forged ahead, Emma, engrossed in the ancient text she held, unwittingly vocalized the ominous warning inscribed within: **"Those who embark on the perilous journey to capture the shadow idol will face a myriad of challenges, including cunningly devised traps lurking in the shadows. Each step forward will be met with the threat of sudden peril, as hidden mechanisms trigger deadly snares and pitfalls designed to ensnare the unwary."**

The tranquility of the forest was shattered by a sudden 'thwung' of a bowstring, followed swiftly by the sharp 'thwack' of an arrow slicing through the air. A venomous projectile whizzed past, embedding itself into the trunk of a nearby tree, narrowly missing Eli by a mere fraction. Startled, the group halted, their senses heightened to the imminent danger surrounding them.

Amelia's sharp eyes swiftly detected the source of the ambush—a barely perceptible tripwire stretched across the path, cunningly concealed amidst the underbrush. With a gasp of realization, she pointed out Eli's unwitting trigger of the mechanism, a testament to the intricate and deadly traps lurking within the forest's depths.

As the fiery orb of the sun dipped below the horizon, casting long shadows across the rugged terrain, the group diligently set about establishing their campsite. Yet, amidst the settling dusk, a haunting chorus of coyote howls pierced the tranquility, echoing through the wilderness with an eerie intensity.

Josh, his senses keenly attuned to the primal symphony of the night, assumed the solemn duty of sentinel, his fingers tightly wrapped around the cold steel of the rifle. With each advancing moment, the distant cries seemed to draw nearer, weaving a sinister tapestry of impending danger.

As the tension mounted, a palpable unease hung heavy in the air, exacerbated by the ominous advance of countless pairs of gleaming eyes that emerged from the shroud of darkness. They formed a spectral tableau, fixated upon the tent and its guardians with an intensity that seemed to pierce the veil between man and beast.

Fearing the worst, Josh hesitated, his grip faltering upon the weapon as he grappled with the uncertainty of the situation. Were these merely ordinary predators, or something more sinister, driven by forces beyond comprehension?

In a desperate bid to assert control, Josh unleashed a blinding torrent of light from his flashlight, a feeble attempt to repel the encroaching menace. Yet, the sudden illumination only served to embolden the pack, igniting a frenzy of snarls and growls as they closed in with savage intent.

Caught off guard by the ferocity of their assault, Josh found himself overwhelmed, his rifle slipping from nerveless fingers as the ravenous creatures descended upon him with a primal fury. His desperate cries for aid rang out into the night, a desperate plea for salvation.

Responding to the urgency of the moment, his companions sprang into action, wielding torches as beacons against the encroaching darkness. With a courage born of necessity, they drove back the relentless tide of fur and fang, forcing the predators to retreat into the shadows.

In the chaos of the struggle, Eli seized upon the fallen rifle, his aim true as he targeted the most imminent threat to Josh's life. With a resounding crack, the shot echoed through the stillness of the night, its deadly trajectory finding its mark with chilling precision.

In the aftermath of the skirmish, a heavy silence descended upon the campsite, broken only by the labored breaths of the survivors. Yet, amidst the carnage, a sense of grim resolve lingered, a testament to the indomitable spirit of humanity in the face of nature's savage fury.

As Emma up to check on Josh, he cried out in pain as a huge portion of his thigh had been wounded in an attempt to fend off the coyotes, and could barely stand. Bandaging the wound, Eli took guard, ordering Josh to go and rest.

VIII

The Forest

As the golden rays of dawn kissed the forest canopy, the group stirred from their makeshift beds, preparing to resume their journey. Amelia, ever vigilant, noticed Eli slumbering in an uncomfortable posture, his head lolling against his rifle.

"Hey, Eli, rise and shine," she prodded him gently. Eli, still lost in the realm of dreams, mumbled a protest, his words muffled by a cascade of drool.

"Five more minutes, mom," he groaned, his voice thick with sleep. Frustrated by his reluctance to awaken, Amelia delivered a swift kick to the rifle, sending Eli tumbling to the ground with a startled yelp.

"Oh my goodness, what a sight!" Amelia exclaimed, her eyes widening in horror at the sight of Eli's face, marred by angry welts left behind by voracious mosquitoes.

As Emily and Josh approached, their concern evident, Emily couldn't suppress a mischievous grin.

"Let's capture this moment forever," Josh suggested, producing a camera and snapping a photo of Eli's afflicted visage.

Dazed and confused, Eli blinked away the remnants of sleep, his confusion mounting as he beheld the laughter of his companions.

"WHAT HAPPENED TO MY FACE?!" he bellowed, scrambling for a mirror to assess the damage, only to be met with raucous laughter from his friends.

After a hearty breakfast, the group resumed their trek towards the fabled Temple of Shadows, Eli's disgruntlement palpable as he swatted furiously at the persistent mosquitoes that seemed intent on making a meal of him.

"Bloodsuckers! Man-eating pests! Vampires!" he cursed, his frustration boiling over as he futilely attempted to ward off the relentless assault of mosquitoes.

"Oh, come now, Eli, they're just hungry," Amelia quipped, her words eliciting chuckles from the group as they pressed onward.

As they reached a clearing, the rhythmic whirr of helicopter rotors sliced through the air, prompting the group to seek refuge beneath the protective canopy of trees to evade detection by potential rescuers. However, Eli, preoccupied with his insect adversaries, unwittingly stumbled into the open, catching the attention of the passing aircraft.

"A kid at three o'clock!" the first officer exclaimed, directing the pilot's attention towards Eli. Acting swiftly, Amelia sprang into action, propelling Eli into a nearby pond to conceal him from view.

As the helicopter circled overhead, the group held their breath, praying to remain unseen. Yet, fate seemed determined to test their resolve as the aircraft doubled back for another pass.

"I swear I saw something!" the first officer insisted, prompting the pilot to initiate another reconnaissance sweep.

Meanwhile, Eli emerged from the pond, waterlogged and utterly bewildered by the commotion.

"What's going on, Amelia?" he inquired, oblivious to the imminent danger.

"They're coming back, we need to hide you," Amelia replied urgently, pushing Eli back into the murky depths of the pond as the helicopter closed in for a second inspection.

"So, are you satisfied now that we've done a second pass?" the pilot inquired of the first officer, a hint of amusement in his voice.

"Mhm," the first officer replied dryly, still uncertain of what he had seen.

"I always knew you needed glasses with a higher number!" teased the pilot, eliciting a terse response from the first officer. "Oh, shut up!" he retorted.

Meanwhile, Amelia hauled Eli out of the pond by his head, exacerbating his already frayed nerves.

"What's the meaning of all this mumbo-jumbo?!" Eli bellowed, his patience worn thin as he demanded an explanation.

As the group continued their trek, Eli was eventually apprised of the situation, his initial anger giving way to a begrudging acceptance of the chaotic circumstances.

As twilight descended upon the forest, the group set about pitching their tents and preparing for supper and much-needed rest. Yet, exhaustion weighed heavily upon them, particularly Emily, who had borne the burden of carrying the injured Josh on her back.

Suddenly, Josh's panicked cry pierced the tranquility of the evening. "A cayman!"

Instantly, the group sprang into action, their senses sharpened by the threat of danger. Amelia tightened her grip on the rifle, her heart racing as she prepared to confront the lurking predator.

But as she steadied her aim, a troubling realization dawned upon her. Caymans didn't inhabit the forests of Maine. With a sinking feeling in her stomach, she realized that they were facing something far more sinister—the nightstalker, stalking them with malevolent intent.

Without hesitation, Amelia reversed her grip on the rifle and charged towards the creature, delivering a powerful blow to its head with the stock. Startled and disoriented, the nightstalker retreated into the darkness, its predatory instincts thwarted by Amelia's swift and decisive action.

"Well, that was easier than I thought," Amelia muttered to herself as she returned to the safety of the tent. With the threat vanquished, the group settled in for the night, grateful for the reprieve from danger and the promise of a peaceful slumber.

IX

Friends?

As the first light of dawn filtered through the dense foliage, the weary adventurers stirred from their slumber within the confines of their tent. Josh, ever the resourceful one, set about preparing breakfast for the group, his culinary efforts interrupted by the sudden rustling of leaves nearby.

Startled by the unexpected disturbance, the group tensed, their minds racing with thoughts of lurking danger. Could the nightstalkers still be lurking in the shadows, their sinister presence lingering in the aftermath of the chaotic night?

Amelia, still groggy from sleep, reclined lazily in the tent, her senses sharpening as she listened intently to the unfolding events. But before they could decipher the source of the disturbance, Eli's attempt to exit the tent resulted in a comical mishap, sending him careening into a bemused Emma who stood just outside.

"Well, that's one way to break the ice! Or maybe in this case, your noses..." Josh quipped, his smile betraying the mischief dancing in his eyes.

Emma, unamused by Josh's jest, retaliated with a swift kick to his uninjured leg, sending him sprawling to the ground with a yelp of surprise.

"Alright, enough bickering, everyone focus!" Eli commanded, his cheeks flushed with embarrassment from his untimely tumble.

As the tension mounted, the rustling of leaves grew louder, heralding the approach of an unexpected visitor. Emerging from the trees with panicked urgency, a majestic moose charged towards them, its wild eyes reflecting a primal fear.

"Get out of the way!" Amelia bellowed, her voice echoing through the forest as she leaped to her feet, her instincts honed by the urgency of the moment. With lightning speed, the moose thundered past them, narrowly missing their tent by a hair's breadth before vanishing into the depths of the wilderness.

From the shadows emerged three figures, their presence commanding attention as they approached with purpose. Armed to the teeth and clad in rugged attire, they exuded an air of authority that demanded respect.

"Identify yourselves!" Amelia commanded, her voice ringing out with unwavering authority as she trained her rifle on the newcomers.

As the figures drew closer, their identities became clear. First among them stood Lucas Shadowmere, a wiry and imposing figure with piercing brown eyes that seemed to bore into the depths of one's soul.

Beside him stood Avery Blackwood, a formidable woman with fiery red hair and steely determination etched upon her features. Clad in practical attire and armed with a rifle, she exuded an aura of fierce independence.

And finally, there was Tristan Blaze, a towering figure with a commanding presence and a gaze as sharp as a blade. With his bald head and weathered countenance, he bore the unmistakable air of a seasoned warrior, his eyepatch a testament to the trials he had endured.

As the trio stood before them, their intentions shrouded in mystery, the group braced themselves for whatever challenges lay ahead, knowing that their encounter with these enigmatic strangers would shape the course of their journey in ways they could scarcely imagine.

As the dust settled from the unexpected encounter with the charging moose, Josh's confusion hung palpably in the air, demanding an explanation for the chaotic spectacle that had just unfolded.

"Uh, would you like to explain... that?" he pointed toward the direction where the moose had disappeared, his tone a mixture of skepticism and curiosity.

Avery, caught off guard by the scrutiny, stammered out a response, her cheeks flushing with embarrassment. "Oh, well, you see, uh... we were trying to get some food and, um... we scared our breakfast away..." she admitted sheepishly, her voice faltering under the weight of awkwardness.

The quartet exchanged skeptical glances, their expressions betraying a lingering doubt. Yet, faced with the trio's earnest explanation, they found themselves reluctantly nodding in begrudging acceptance.

"Eh... makes sense," they chimed in unison, their skepticism tempered by the sheer absurdity of the situation.

With the tension diffused, the trio closed in on the quartet, their demeanor shifting from awkwardness to urgency as they broached the subject of their shared destination.

"Are you guys also headed to the Temple of Shadows?" Tristan inquired, his voice carrying a sense of gravitas that commanded attention.

Amelia, still processing the revelation, responded with a mixture of surprise and suspicion. "How do you guys know?" she demanded, her eyes narrowing as she scrutinized the newcomers.

"We come from the neighboring town of Summerbrooks," Tristan explained, his tone somber with the weight of tragedy. "The nightstalkers have completely destroyed our town. We need your help to take us there and contain them."

As the implications of Tristan's words sank in, the quartet realized that their journey had taken on a newfound urgency. With the fate of Summerbrooks hanging in the balance, they knew that their path was now inexorably intertwined with that of the trio, bound together by a common purpose and a shared quest for justice.

As the day wore on, the quartet of Josh, Amelia, Emma, and Eli found themselves bolstered by the addition of three more allies, swelling their ranks with newfound support for their journey ahead. With the sun sinking low on the horizon, casting long shadows across the forest floor, both groups of adventurers sought refuge in a secluded clearing, where they pitched their tents and prepared for the night to come.

After a hearty meal and lively conversation around the crackling fire, the group settled into their respective sleeping bags, the warmth of camaraderie chasing away the chill of the night air. Eli, ever vigilant, tended to the fire, feeding it with fresh logs to ward off the encroaching darkness and the lurking threat of nightstalkers.

As he busied himself with the task, his keen eyes caught sight of something glinting in the firelight—a crumpled piece of paper, nestled among the embers. Intrigued, he reached out and retrieved it, a sense of déjà vu washing over him as he recognized the familiar script upon its weathered surface.

It bore a striking resemblance to one of the pages from the ancient tome that Emma had unearthed in her Meemaw's attic, its yellowed edges and faded ink hinting at untold secrets and hidden mysteries. With a furrowed brow, Eli unfolded the paper and began to read, his unease growing with each passing word.

"If a person reaches the Temple of Shadows and makes peace with the nightstalkers, one can become unimaginably powerful, becoming the leader of the nightstalkers, with such intense control over the creatures... it's a path fraught with peril."

With trembling hands, he read aloud the ominous message:

"In the depths of darkness, where shadows reign, Lies the Temple of Shadows, where power wanes. Beware the allure of its whispered promises, For within its halls, lies the seeds of crisis.

To seek its power is to court one's demise, For the nightstalkers' embrace holds no disguise. Choose wisely, for the path you tread, For the light you seek may lead to dread."

as he went to sleep, he decided to keep the paper safe to show the group the next day.

X

The power

The morning sun cast its golden rays upon the campsite, illuminating the weary faces of the adventurers as they gathered around Eli, who wasted no time in revealing the mysterious piece of paper he had discovered amidst the remnants of the previous night's fire. As he unfolded the crumpled parchment, its weathered edges and faded ink seemed to hold the weight of untold secrets, its presence casting a shadow of unease upon the group.

But as Eli presented the paper to his companions, a strange tension settled over the trio of Lucas, Avery, and Tristan, their expressions shifting from curiosity to discomfort in the blink of an eye. Their furtive glances and uneasy shuffling betrayed a sense of guilt, as if they were hiding something that they wished had remained buried.

"Where did you find that?" Lucas demanded, his voice tinged with disbelief as he snatched the paper from Eli's outstretched hand, his fingers trembling slightly as he examined the cryptic message scrawled upon its surface.

"It was just lying there," Eli replied nonchalantly, gesturing towards the extinguished but still-smoking campfire where the mysterious artifact had been discovered. Yet, even as he spoke, a nagging sense of doubt gnawed at his conscience, whispering of hidden truths and concealed motives.

Sensing the growing tension, Josh interjected with a lighthearted jest, his attempt to diffuse the atmosphere met with chuckles from the group. "Anyways, let's get going," he declared with a grin, his jovial demeanor masking the underlying unease that lingered beneath the surface.

As Eli set about firing up the campfire and preparing breakfast for the group, the air was thick with unspoken tension, the weight of their shared secret hanging heavy in the air. Yet, amidst the mundane tasks of camp life, disaster struck in the most unexpected of ways.

In a moment of carelessness, Avery stumbled over a wayward vine, her graceful stride abruptly interrupted as she careened into Eli, sending them both tumbling towards the blazing fire. With a cry of alarm, Eli leapt to his feet, his eyes ablaze with fury as he confronted the hapless perpetrator of their near-miss.

"Are you out of your mind, you brainless baboon?!" he roared, his voice echoing through the forest as he fixed Avery with a withering glare. In that tense moment, the simmering tensions that had lain dormant within the group threatened to boil over, their fragile alliance teetering on the brink of collapse.

As the morning sun climbed higher into the sky, casting its warm embrace upon the forest below, the adventurers found themselves ensnared in a web of secrets and lies, their journey fraught with peril and uncertainty. And as they prepared to venture forth into the unknown, the weight of their shared burden hung heavy upon their shoulders, a constant reminder of the dangers that lurked just beyond the edge of their vision.

With the tension momentarily diffused, Emma took charge, her voice cutting through the lingering unease like a clarion call to action. "Come on, let's get going," she commanded, her tone firm and resolute. "We don't have all day."

Her words galvanized the group into motion, stirring them from their reverie and igniting a renewed sense of purpose within their hearts. With determined strides, they gathered their belongings and prepared to set forth on their journey to the Temple of Shadows, their eyes fixed upon the horizon with unwavering resolve.

As they ventured deeper into the heart of the forest, each step brought them closer to their destiny, their path illuminated by the faint glimmer of hope that flickered within their souls.

And as they embarked upon the next leg of their journey, the echoes of their footsteps reverberated through the ancient woods, a testament to their unwavering determination and unyielding spirit. For they knew that their path would be fraught with peril and uncertainty, but they marched onward nonetheless, guided by the light of their shared purpose and the promise of a brighter tomorrow.

XI

The Temple of Shadows

"There," declared Amelia, her voice laced with anticipation, as she pointed toward a distant cascade that tumbled gracefully from the heights of a sheer cliff. "That waterfall marks our path to the temple. Once we cross it, our destination shall be within reach."

With determination etched upon his features, Eli swiftly took charge, deftly employing a grappling hook tethered to a sturdy rope, which he skillfully launched across the chasm to secure it upon a weathered boulder jutting from the opposite bank.

With unwavering resolve, Amelia took the lead, her gaze fixed upon the tumultuous waters below as she poised herself at the precipice, preparing to brave the dizzying cross. With each heartbeat echoing in her ears, sherossed above the abyss, suspended amidst a swirling vortex of froth and spray, until at last, she emerged victorious upon the far shore, her heart pounding with exhilaration.

One by one, the rest of the group followed suit, their movements fueled by a mixture of trepidation and determination. Yet, as Emma neared the halfway point, a deafening crack shattered the tranquility, reverberating through the canyon like a thunderclap.

In an instant and a sickening snap, the rope gave way, severed by Tristan's knife. Emma hurtled earthward. Horror etched upon their faces, the group watched in helpless disbelief as Emma disappeared into the roiling depths below, swallowed by the voracious maw of the chasm.

"WHY DID YOU DO THAT?!" Eli's voice thundered with fury, his eyes blazing with a mixture of anger and disbelief as he confronted Tristan, demanding an answer for his treacherous act. But as the words left his lips, a chilling sound pierced the air—the ominous cocking of two guns.

Whirling around, Eli's heart sank as he beheld Lucas and Avery standing before them, their weapons trained unwaveringly upon him, Josh, and Amelia. Betrayal hung heavy in the air, a bitter taste that soured the camaraderie they had once shared.

"Traitors!" Eli spat the word like venom, his mind reeling with the enormity of their deceit. How could they have been so blind, so naive to trust these newfound allies?

"You children are so dumb," Tristan sneered, his voice dripping with contempt as he raised his own weapon to join the others. "We used you, kid, to help us find the way to the temple to lead the nightstalkers, not to capture them, and you believed us."

The realization hit Eli like a physical blow, the weight of their deception crushing his spirit. They had been played for fools, manipulated by their own desire for truth and justice. And now, as they stood on the precipice of betrayal, there was no escape from the harsh reality of their situation.

Amidst the chaos and despair, Josh sought to console the distraught Amelia, his words a feeble attempt to assuage the anguish that gripped her soul. Meanwhile, Eli, his gaze fixed upon the yawning abyss, strained to discern any sign of their fallen comrade amidst the tumultuous waters below, his heart heavy with a sense of profound loss and regret.

"Emma, are you there? Please, answer me!" Eli's desperate plea echoed through the silent canyon, reverberating off the sheer walls in a haunting chorus of unanswered questions. But all he received in return were the cold, mocking echoes of his own voice, bouncing back to him with cruel indifference.

His heart pounding with fear and uncertainty, Eli strained his ears for any sign of a response, any glimmer of hope that his friend might still be alive. But the oppressive silence hung heavy around him, suffocating him with its deafening absence.

"Emma!" he called out again, his voice cracking with desperation as he searched frantically for any sign of her presence. But there was nothing, only the empty expanse of the canyon stretching out before him.

"Oh, come on, please stop the drama," taunted Tristan, his voice dripping with mockery as he approached Eli, a sinister glint in his eyes. "If you miss her so much, let us help you meet her again."

Before Eli could react, Tristan grabbed him roughly and hurled him into the abyss of the waterfall, his body tumbling through the air with sickening speed. With a cry of alarm, Amelia and Josh were dragged along with him, their screams lost amidst the roar of rushing water.

Preparing for the inevitable impact, the trio braced themselves as they collided with the churning stream below, their bodies tossed and turned by the tumultuous current before finally coming to rest on a rocky outcrop nearby.

As the world swam back into focus, Josh blinked in disbelief, his eyes widening as he spotted Emma kneeling beside him, her face filled with concern. "What the heck, Emma? How are you still alive?" he blurted out, unable to comprehend the miraculous sight before him.

As the others stirred from unconsciousness, Emma explained how she swung and fell behind the wall of the waterfall quite on accident, and told others to follow her to check it out. One by one, all crossed the waterfall and arrived at the cavity where Emma had landed.

However, as Eli leaped into the hidden alcove, he found himself ensnared by a tangled web of vines, his momentum abruptly halted as he tumbled forward, landing unceremoniously amidst the confines of the cavern. Blinking away the disorientation, he found himself face-to-face with an ancient skeleton, its hollow gaze fixed upon him with a macabre intensity.

Regaining his composure, Eli attempted to lighten the mood with a jest, his words tinged with nervous annoyance. "Well, that's certainly a certain way to welcome people," he quipped, delivering a kick to the skull of the skeletal sentinel, sending it soaring through the air like a wayward football. Yet, despite his attempt at levity, the unsettling presence of the forgotten remains served as a stark reminder of the perils that lurked within the depths of the forest.

As their exploration led them deeper into the labyrinthine depths of the cavern, they emerged into a vast and solemn chamber, its walls adorned with intricate carvings of a bygone era. "Look! The very entity we've been confronting, immortalized in these ancient artworks," exclaimed Emma, her voice reverent as she pointed to a particularly striking depiction. "And there, behold the figure clutching the idol," she continued, her eyes alight with excitement. "This must be the heart of the temple, the culmination of our journey!"

With a torch ablaze to ward off the encroaching darkness, the group pressed onward, their footsteps echoing through the hallowed halls as they ventured deeper into the sanctum. Entering a chamber shrouded in shadow, they were suddenly ensnared as the heavy doors slammed shut behind them, sealing their fate within the bowels of the temple.

A faint murmur heralded the onset of a dire threat, as water surged forth from unseen conduits, flooding the chamber with a relentless deluge. Panic seized the hearts of the trapped adventurers as they struggled against the rising tide, their precious air rapidly dwindling in the suffocating embrace of the submerged chamber.

With grim determination, Josh's gaze fixated upon a valve nestled amidst the swirling currents, a glimmer of hope amidst the encroaching despair. "I must act swiftly to release the pressure and stem the tide!" he declared, his resolve unyielding as he plunged into the icy embrace of the rising waters.

As the water extinguished the flickering flame of their torch, plunging the chamber into stygian darkness, Amelia joined the frantic search for their valiant companion. Yet, amidst the murky depths, Josh remained elusive, his presence obscured by the inky blackness that enveloped them.

Suddenly, a resounding creak shattered the oppressive silence, signaling the release of pent-up pressure as the valve yielded to Josh's efforts. With a rush of displaced water, the chamber was spared from its watery tomb, the torrential deluge receding as swiftly as it had come.

XII

The Shadow Idol

As the group basked in the glow of their success, their jubilation was cut short by Emma's sharp cry of warning. "WAIT!" she screamed, her voice echoing through the now accessible torch-lit chamber. Eli froze in his tracks, his hand hovering inches from the beckoning hallway ahead.

"The hallway is too empty, it must be booby-trapped!" Emma's words rang out with urgency, a stark reminder of the dangers that lay ahead. With a quick, decisive motion, she grabbed a nearby stick and pressed it against the tiled floor, only to watch in horror as it plummeted into a hidden chasm below, its descent punctuated by the ominous sound of spikes meeting stone.

Undeterred by the peril that lurked around every corner, the group pressed on, their senses heightened by the looming threat of danger. But even their vigilance was no match for the cunning traps that lay in wait, as evidenced by the sudden snap of a pressure crossbow that caught Emma off guard.

With a cry of pain, she staggered backwards, clutching her wounded arm as blood seeped from the fresh wound. In a heartbeat, Josh was by her side, his eyes scanning the protruding tip of the arrow with a mixture of concern and relief.

"It's not poisoned," he declared, his words a welcome reassurance amidst the chaos that surrounded them. With Emma's injury tended to as best they could, the group pressed forward, their determination unyielding in the face of adversity.

Dodging each trap with practiced precision, they navigated the treacherous corridors with a mix of caution and courage, their eyes fixed on the prize that lay ahead—the shadow idol, gleaming dully in the torchlight at the far end of the grand hall.

As Eli staggered towards the shadow idol, his hand outstretched to claim the coveted prize, a sudden explosion shattered the air, the deafening roar of gunfire echoing through the chamber. With a cry of pain, Eli stumbled backwards, his hands clutching his abdomen where a bullet had struck him with brutal force, sending waves of agony coursing through his body.

As he writhed in pain on the cold stone floor, a familiar voice cut through the chaos, dripping with malice and contempt. "We meet again," sneered Tristan, his figure looming ominously amidst the billowing smoke, his gun trained unwaveringly upon Eli's prone form. "Looks like your guardian angel was on duty when I chucked you down the cliff, huh?"

With a mocking laugh, he raised his weapon higher, his eyes gleaming with sadistic glee. "Don't worry," he taunted, his voice dripping with venom. "I'll make sure he doesn't need to be on duty anymore."

But before Tristan could pull the trigger, a blur of motion hurtled towards him, knocking him off balance and causing his shot to go wide. It was Josh, his face a mask of determination as he launched himself at their assailant, his fists flying in a flurry of blows.

With a roar of rage, Emma and Amelia joined the fray, their bodies moving with fluid grace as they fought tooth and nail against their treacherous adversaries. The chamber erupted into chaos as punches were thrown and bodies collided, the sound of grunts and curses mingling with the clatter of weapons and the crackle of magic.

In the midst of the melee, Eli struggled to his feet, his vision swimming with pain as he fought to regain his bearings. With a fierce determination burning in his eyes, he joined his friends in the battle, his fists clenched tight as he faced off against the forces of darkness that threatened to consume them all.

For in that moment, as the echoes of their struggle reverberated through the chamber, they knew that they were fighting not just for their lives, but for the fate of the world itself. And as they clashed against their enemies with unyielding resolve, they vowed to stand together, united against the darkness that sought to tear them apart.

As the chaos of battle raged on, Josh's quick reflexes allowed him to seize control of Tristan's gun, holding him, Avery, and Lucas at gunpoint. But in a desperate bid to reclaim his weapon, Tristan made a sudden move, prompting Josh to instinctively pull the trigger. With a deafening bang, Tristan fell lifeless to the ground, his demise marking a grim turn in the already perilous situation.

Before the group could react, a bloodcurdling screech pierced the air, followed by a thunderous roar as a horde of nightstalkers descended upon Avery and Lucas, their savage claws tearing through flesh and bone with merciless efficiency. Caught off guard, the traitorous pair met a grisly end, their screams drowned out by the frenzied onslaught of their monstrous assailants.

Seizing the opportunity to escape, the group fled the scene, their hearts pounding with adrenaline as they raced through the treacherous corridors of the temple. With Eli still bleeding profusely from his wound, Emma and Josh lent their support, their determination unshaken despite the odds stacked against them.

Finally arriving in the ritual chamber, the group scattered across the room, each member taking their designated position as outlined in the ancient tome. With trembling hands, they placed the shadow idol at the center of the room, its dark surface pulsating with an otherworldly energy.

As they began to chant the sacred incantations written in the book, a sense of anticipation filled the air, mingling with the lingering echoes of battle that still reverberated through the chamber. With each word spoken, the idol began to glow with an intense radiance, its power growing stronger with every passing moment.

And then, with a blinding flash of light, the idol levitated into the air, its dark aura enveloping the chamber in an ethereal glow. As if drawn by some unseen force, the free nightstalkers were pulled inexorably towards the idol, their forms dissolving into the abyss of darkness that lay within.

With a final surge of power, the idol sealed shut, trapping the nightstalkers within its depths for all eternity. And as the last echoes of their screams faded into silence, a profound sense of relief washed over the group, their victory hard-won but undeniably sweet.

XIII

The End?

As they emerged from the dense jungle, relief washed over the weary adventurers as they beheld the reassuring sight of a helicopter circling overhead, its presence a beacon of rescue amidst the wilderness. With a wave of determination, Amelia stepped forward, signaling for the aircraft to descend and offer them passage to safety.

With a whirring of blades, the helicopter touched down upon the forest floor, its doors swinging open to welcome the weary travelers aboard. As they climbed aboard and settled into their seats, a sense of profound gratitude washed over them, knowing that their ordeal was finally at an end.

As the helicopter soared skyward, leaving the shadowed canopy behind, Crestwood loomed on the horizon like a promised haven, its familiar streets a testament to the comforts of home and the warmth of familial embrace.

Upon their arrival, tears of joy flowed freely as parents rushed forward to envelop their children in tearful hugs, their relief palpable as they welcomed their loved ones back into their arms.

Amidst the joyful reunion, the intrepid quartet looked to the future with newfound resolve, ready to embrace the ordinary rhythms of life after their extraordinary journey. Yet, as they basked in the glow of their hard-won victory, a nagging sense of unease lingered in the depths of their minds, a silent question that dared to challenge the newfound peace they had secured.

As they celebrated their triumphant return to Crestwood, the air was filled with a palpable sense of relief and joy. Yet beneath the surface, the echoes of their harrowing ordeal lingered like a shadow, a constant reminder of the dangers that lurked in the darkness.

Even as they reveled in their hard-won victory, the whispers of the unknown whispered ominously in the wind, a haunting reminder that the shadows they had left behind may yet cast their pall upon their lives once more. But for now, they chose to bask in the warmth of their success, finding solace in the bonds of friendship that had carried them through the darkest of times.

But amidst the joyous celebrations, there was also a somber note of loss. For while Emma, Amelia, and Josh went on to fully recover from their injuries, the same could not be said for Eli. Despite the best efforts of the medical team, he ultimately succumbed to his wounds in the hospital, leaving behind a void that could never be filled.

Yet even in death, Eli's courage and sacrifice would not be forgotten. All four of them were bravely honored all over the nation, their names immortalized in the annals of history as heroes who had stood against the forces of darkness and emerged victorious. And as their story spread far and wide, they received immense recognition, their bravery serving as a beacon of hope for all who faced the perils of the unknown.

As they stood amidst the embrace of their loved ones, the echoes of their past adventures resonated in their minds, leaving them to wonder: Is their newfound peace truly secure, or do darker forces lurk on the horizon, waiting to test their mettle once again? Only time would tell.

www.ingramcontent.com/pod-product-compliance
Lightning Source LLC
Chambersburg PA
CBHW020515160726
47991CB00007B/2965